The Bread Fairy

Dawna Pederzani

AuthorHouse™
1663 Liberty Drive
Bloomington, IN 47403
www.authorhouse.com
Phone: 1 (833) 262-8899

This book is printed on acid-free paper.

ISBN: 978-1-7283-7255-6 (sc)
ISBN: 978-1-7283-7256-3 (hc)
ISBN: 978-1-7283-7254-9 (e)

Library of Congress Control Number: 2020916765

Print information available on the last page.

Published by AuthorHouse 11/05/2020

authorHOUSE®

To my daughter, Liana, born weighing one pound seven ounces. Now she sports blue hair, a sharp wit, and a keen artistic talent. It was Liana who identified Bread Fairy as the perfect name for Mary Jane. Through sheer grit, Liana has weathered her storms with grace and continues to do so today.

To my son, Miguel, who in his short life has faced challenges that would have flattened most of us. His wit, charm, and ability to love serve as an example to others of the power of resilience.

To the late Matt Drummy, a writing professor extraordinaire. Matt encouraged, cajoled, begged, and pleaded for me to get out of legal classes and enroll somewhere—anywhere—to study writing. He knew how to take a match to a smoldering idea and blow it into greatness. Matt was a kind and caring man who sadly was consumed by his own internal fire. I hope that he hears my conversations with him from time to time.

Times were different and really hard. They became
that way suddenly and without warning.

One day, life was pretty good with room for only a few minor
complaints (from a ten-year-old's perspective).

School was in session, friends were playing outside, after-
school programs were in gear, and the much-anticipated
softball season was just around the corner.

Then suddenly, it seemed as if life itself was being canceled, one activity and one life event at a time until there was little that was familiar or fun remaining. It seemed like everyone was at a dance, joyful and carefree, then suddenly the music stopped playing.

Something called coronavirus, a terrible sickness, had found its way to the United States from other countries. Like paint spilling over a big ball, randomly and quickly, it engulfed every country in its path.

More sadly, this virus was causing hundreds of thousands of people to fall gravely ill and many to die. All were ordered to stay in their homes and practice social distancing—that meant staying six feet away from everyone, even friends and family who didn't live in the same house. Life as we knew it was being washed down a giant drain, never to be seen again.

Pets were safe to be around, including the fifteen dogs that Delia had saved from death and now housed at her rescue, which was also her home. There was no social distancing needed there and thank goodness! A face full of fur and a random face cleaning by a wet tongue were welcome reminders that good still existed. The animals also lifted everyone's mood.

Virginia, Delia's daughter, had blue hair. Blue like the ocean! Blue like the sky on a perfect Vermont day. Blue like that awful window cleaner that people use. Delia would not use that cleaner because she knew it had been tested on animals, causing them horrible pain, blindness, and even death.

Delia taught Virginia at an early age to look for the bunny symbol on containers, which showed that that kind of testing had not been done on the product.

Anyway, Virginia had teal-blue hair, a wit that could slap the happy out of a morning in lightning-short order, an amazing talent for art, and a distaste for politicians. "Surely it is carried in my female DNA," Virginia would say with a bit of prideful gleam in her eye.

Virginia had opinions galore about who was steering the broken ship of her country and was more than happy to tell anyone with the time to listen. Virginia had autism, which lowered her filter and allowed the crack in her wit to have an extra sting, though she didn't notice. Those who knew and loved her got it and didn't generally take offense to it. Those who didn't could not imagine such sharpness going unchecked.

This was most likely why Delia had chosen to be a foster parent thirty years ago. Her friends had tried to discourage her. They said it would be hard; it was. They said it would be painful emotionally; it was. They said it would ruin Delia's life. It did not. In fact, even with all the struggles, pain, and challenges, being a foster parent made Delia and her life better. She became stronger, clearer, and unafraid of being an advocate for a child in her care.

To be fair, it was pretty darned hard for Virginia. She had to watch the challenging behaviors and hear the arguing and sometimes worse when some children would use bad words or become physical with her mother. She struggled with this invasion and often hid in her art or books or video games.

Even when she was a child, Delia had had little room for larger-than-life imaginary characters. She didn't care for superheroes, and Cinderella should have her head examined for dressing up, making up, and waiting for some ridiculously plastic-looking prince to fix her life. After all, housecleaning and singing would accomplish so much more in the way of order and calm. More importantly, packing up those nasty sisters and moving them on would bring a lot of positivity and satisfaction.

Delia was practical, and so she saved talk of heroes for actual heroes—
those who earned that title fair and square. The word *exceptional*
was rarely used as it was intended. Little was exceptional, and what
was, deserved the parking spot right in front of the door, not one
in a line with fifty others. Delia knew exceptional when she saw it.
Exceptional was a selfless act from one human toward another, an
act that provided no tangible benefit to the person performing it.

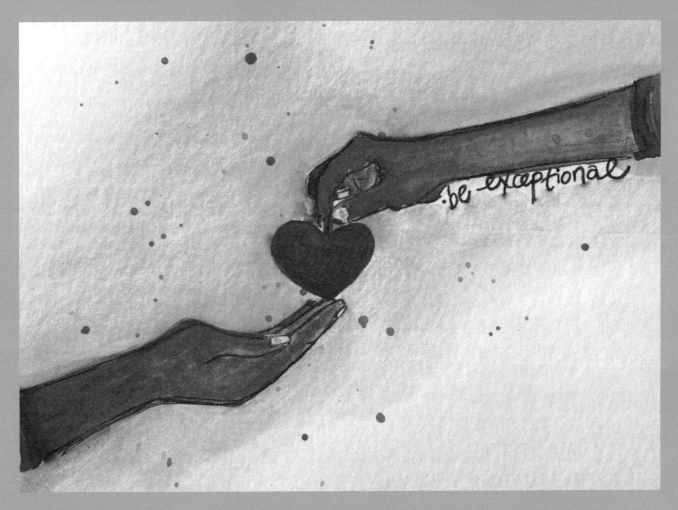

It could be saving a dog who had been tossed aside and was shut down and angry. Maybe that dog was even willing to bite if its warning growl was ignored.

What thing, what moment, could be identified as exceptional? That might be an open-pawed leap into Delia's arms made by Maddie, a little poodle once frozen with fear; a tender and nearly missed lick on the hand from little Pam, a scruffy terrier more prone to running than hugging; or an all-out landslide of flesh onto her person by a 130-pound mastiff named Sasha. Those moments were exceptional.

The depth of feeling and connection was always evident to Virginia when she saw the tightly held tears and raspy voice that punctuated her mother trying to hide those tender moments, holding them in a safe and private place. It was usually a failed attempt, as these dogs had her mother's heart.

· Maddie ·

· Pam ·

· Sasha ·

One way to seek connection during this time of isolation was through a local online community called Front Door Welcome. Delia would log on daily to read about the happenings of the community, the changing landscape of health issues, business closings, musings and the poetry of people tethered to their computers.

There were political rants, neighbors complaining about something, and thankfully neighbors offering help or goods to share. Occasionally there would be the sharing of a selfless and tender act, a human trying to weave a beautiful quilt out of some tattered and dirty remnants.

That was what this pandemic left us—a tattered landscape and dirtied lens through which to view our changed world, towns, relationships, and even homes. It was hard and sometimes just depressing.

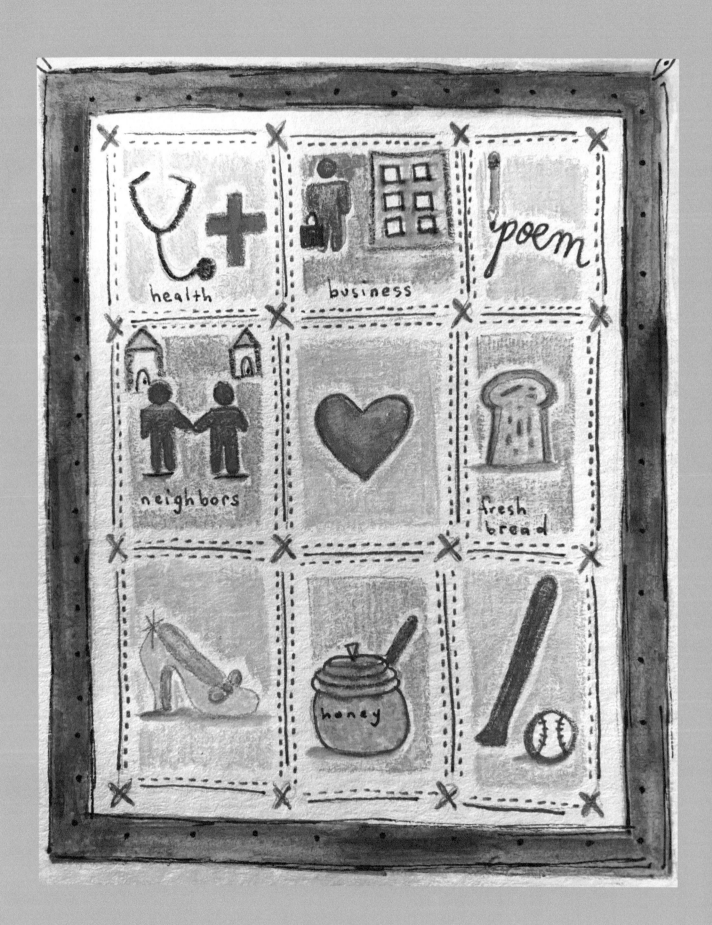

health

business

poem

neighbors

fresh bread

honey

Then one evening on Front Door Welcome, Delia saw a
post from Mary Jane and her husband, Steve.

"My husband and I are avid from-scratch bread makers and would love to make
homemade bread for those who are quarantined in their homes or otherwise
not able to get to grocery stores easily. Please email me your name, phone
number, and address, and we will call or text the night before your name is
up! If we have already delivered a loaf to you and you would like another this
next week, please let us know, as people and situations can change
from week to week. If you need an emergency loaf, please let
us know, and we will do our best to get it to you ASAP!"

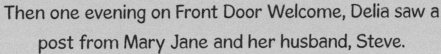

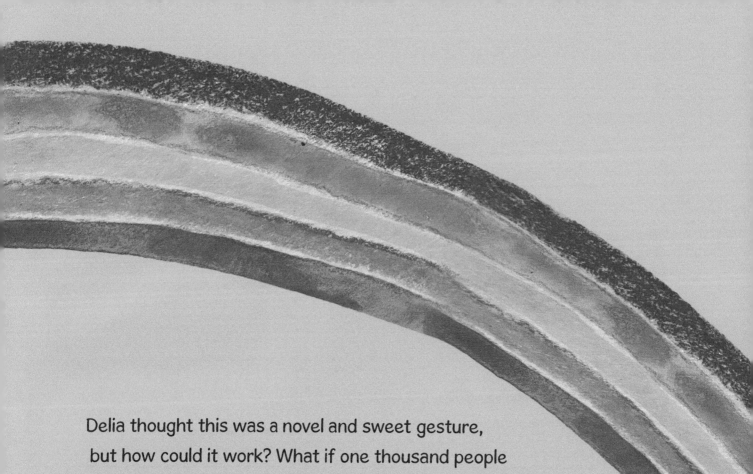

Delia thought this was a novel and sweet gesture,
but how could it work? What if one thousand people
wanted homemade bread? Would they get it? For how long?

This could not be true. It was just some spur-of-the-
moment Cinderella kind of thing. The shoe never fit. But, Delia
thought, there was no harm in asking. And so she wrote a reply.

"A warm loaf of bread during this sad, scary, and lonely
time would be so welcome. Thank you."

Delia expected nothing. Surely those one thousand bread lovers had not only
emptied the shelves but taken even the plans and thoughts for more bread
from this couple's minds. This was a no-win situation, but she had tried.

The next day an email arrived with the subject line "Bread." This was going to be it—the note that began with "We are so sorry ..."

But it did not. In fact, they thanked Delia for writing.

"We have wheat, light wheat, and white (our favorite, tinged with honey)."

That was it! Delia firmly applied the brakes and put her order in—honey white, please! Mary Jane replied that the loaf would appear in a couple of days and that a text would be sent announcing its arrival.

To a bread lover—and Delia was one—this was akin to the pumpkin carriage being pulled by two white horses arriving to take her to the carbohydrate ball. Bring on the bread!

Delia was in the kennel feeding dogs when a volunteer said, "Do you know you have a loaf of bread sitting in your entryway?"

"Get out!" Delia yelled as she leaped for the door. This was a rare kind of magical moment when something that was promised was actually delivered. These moments were rare for Delia, and she embraced them with enthusiasm.

Virginia came out, blue hair gleaming in the bright sunlight, with shock and satisfaction on her face at the sight of the bread. She too had wondered.

And so, sitting on the front step, warm bread in hand and volunteers gathered with wonder, Delia shared the story. Volunteers marveled. They wanted to see and feel this warm and weighty loaf. They wanted to smell its goodness. Who were they kidding? They wanted to eat it up!

Everyone went to the dining room, talking about the bread, its warm, sweet goodness, and the people who made it and delivered it. They had kept a promise to a stranger out of pure kindness. This one gesture brought out such joy.

Virginia said, "Now we have a bread fairy!" This lovely couple had been christened Mr. and Mrs. Bread Fairy. How would Delia let them know?

This lovely exchange of text messages, followed by the arrival of warm bread, continued every Tuesday like clockwork. Each exchange was a sweet and magical happening, and each loaf was happily shared with everyone present. The only thing that was missing in this process was that Delia had yet to meet Mary Jane. She was elusive. Her comings and goings were lightning quick, stealthily quiet, and absolutely void of someone seeking praise—the giving was all the thanks she needed. Delia, wanting a human face with which to connect this exchange, was determined to meet this caring person. But how? She was often so busy and distracted, only to discover the gift after the fact. This would take planning.

The following Tuesday, Delia waited inside the front door quiet as she could be. *Ping* ... the text came saying that the arrival of a loaf of bread was imminent. This week it was to be sourdough! Oh how Delia enjoyed a tangy bite of good sourdough! Quietly but quickly, Delia opened the front door. There, wide eyed, stood a small, blond woman with a kind face and huge smile, holding the basket with the loaf of bread. It struck Delia as curious that the person her mind had envisioned as larger-than-life seemed quite child-like as she stood on the walk. Startled and stumbling for words, Delia and Mary Jane laughed before chatting, both glad to have finally met.

That evening, Delia posted on Front Door Welcome:

"The bread fairy is truly real! Today was delivery day. As always, she sent me a text announcing her arrival. This time, I wanted a peek. I waited inside the door and, as soon as I heard the ping of her text, opened the door slowly, and there she was, goods still in hand! It was like Christmas, with cookies and milk placed ceremoniously for Mr. Claus, but even better. Thank you, Bread Fairy. Even though we met and spoke, I will still imagine those yummy, warm and fragrant loaves just appearing like magic!"

Mary Jane emailed a heartfelt thank you.

It would be Easter soon, but there would be no family celebrations, no closeness, no hugs, and no church gatherings. Society would have to dig deep to find a new norm, a new way of saying and showing it.

On Good Friday, Delia was making an early-morning senior outing for essentials. While standing at the checkout, she noticed stacks of hot cross buns. She decided that she wanted some special Easter traditions. They looked inviting, but Delia opened her phone and did some research. She read about spices and candied fruit, such as leaf-green cherries and chunks of pineapple so yellow they made the sun look dim. Those buns were the things of fruitcake nightmares! She moved on.

That night she asked her friends if they had ever eaten those buns; none of them had ever touched those things. Delia decided that she would just let the buns go as one of life's missed opportunities—
or perhaps an instance of dodging that green cherry bullet!

x hot cross buns x

On Easter Sunday, there was a knock at Delia's door. She opened it and saw that it was not the Easter Bunny or the Rookies Dinosaur, who would arrive later to dance on the front lawn and deliver awesome craft root beer. It was the bread fairy, and what did she have? She had homemade hot cross buns.

Delia was dumbfounded. How could that be? They had not spoken. Delia had not posted her description and close call with hot cross buns at the store and they had no fairy friends in common! Yet there in the bag were beautiful hot cross buns. The bread fairy announced that she does not like fluorescent fruit and so had substituted raisins and currants and hoped that deviation from the traditional recipe was ok. The same friends and volunteers who were Delia's sounding board about the buns in the store were at her house for Easter dinner. They were shocked and envious!

The buns were a hit, and everyone was grateful.

Behind the socially conscious and caring bread fairy was Steve. Mary Jane described him as her husband, her wonderful muse, and her cheerleader in almost everything she did. That was exceptional! Steve carved beautiful hearts into every loaf of bread. This was his way of sending extra love to every bread fairy recipient.

. hand carved hearts ♥
in every loaf .

A lot can come from suffering, isolation, and challenge. Everything about life has been altered, and yet there is humor. Delia saw a man who used pool noodles to make a headdress that measured six feet long. They hung off his head as a colorful warning to keep others at a safe distance.

In the space of a week, Delia adopted out nearly all the eighteen dogs staying with her that had never known a safe, loving, and happy home; even better, the bread fairy was born. Even through darkness, light can be seen.

Shine on, bread fairy!

About the Author

Dawna Pederzani is a lover of animals, an artist, and a writer. She is a tireless advocate for children with special needs, including her own and the ones whom she has fostered over the past thirty years. Dawna operates two nonprofit dog rescues with the help of some loving and dedicated volunteers. Together, they rescue, rehabilitate, and rehome hundreds of neglected, abandoned, and abused dogs from many parts of the United States. She lives in Vermont with her two children, who have overcome enormous obstacles to become their full and creative selves, and her three English bulldogs, Peter, Lulubelle, and Buttercup.

About the Book

The treachery called COVID-19, a deadly virus spreading in a pandemic, has risen from its sleep. It is a voracious beast and is devouring all that we know to be normal. People are afraid, sad, lonely, and confused. There is little to be hopeful about or thankful for—that is, until one lady has an idea born of caring for others and their well-being and reaches out through a public forum. Her idea is basic: everyone needs food. Food is a connection, a binder of experience. And so the bread fairy is born.

Kate Cahill Vansuch

Kate Cahill Vansuch lived in Vermont for fourteen years. She volunteered at the Vermont English Bulldog Rescue with her daughter and adopted a beautiful bulldog from VEBR. She is a nurse and an artist and currently lives near Philadelphia with her family.

Mary Jane Dieter and Husband Steve

Mary Jane Dieter is the inspiration behind the story and in fact is the Bread Fairy. Steve is her husband, muse and heart carver decoration in each loaf adding a level of love that is so.much appreciated

Printed in the United States
By Bookmasters